# Mongrel
*Short Stories*

Edited by: Dustin Brewer

toasty press

To those willing to look past pedigree.

# CONTENTS

# INTRODUCTION

Mongrel is a word with a variety of meanings. 'Just a mongrel,' someone might say, referring to dog of unidentifiable breed trotting by the side of the road. Or, in an even more derogatory way, a person of mixed ancestry might be unkindly called the same. To me, however, the word mongrel connotes warmth as I think of a friend of mine who has agreed to let his image be used on the cover of this book on condition that a cut of the proceeds be used to buy his favorite treats. And, I can assure you, they will be. Like my friend, this short story collection is made up of a variety of parts that may at first seem like they don't fit together. Settings range from a tiny town in Montana, to a big-city restaurant, and also to an office building, among others. But now that they have come together, I think that the short stories in this collection create a lovely mix. They are a mongrel, like my friend.

You'll find four stories written by me (D.B.) between 2019 and 2022. And to introduce some hybrid vigor to this collection, you'll also find a story by Olympia Bernes (O.B.) and another by Jacob Brewer (J.B.). As I enter my fourth decade, I've found that feelings don't flow as freely as they used to. Less situations have the wings of novelty and more callouses form every day, thus threatening to dull my experience. Reading and writing, more than most things, help to keep me feeling. Imagining helps me to remain excited and to stay alive, in the soulful sense of the word. I'm certain that I'm not alone in this relationship with words and so hope that this mongrel of a short story collection helps you feel in ways that no one story, or author, could have conjured alone.

Dustin Brewer
Mt. Pleasant, Michigan
1.1.23

*Mountains*

by

D.B.

"Miyuki, it is a real pleasure to meet you," Dan Forster said, shaking her hand. The one which wasn't missing two fingers.

"The pleasure's mine," she said, as they sat down in the coffee shop, making an odd pair. Middle-aged man, balding, thick glasses, and collared shirt. Blue jeans, beer belly. Joined by a young woman, colorful and expensive tattoos spilling from beneath her tank-top and spiraling around her arms. Nose-ring, yoga pants. Muscles.

"Tell me a bit about you, before we begin." Her voice was cheery, smile big, and stare cold.

"OK. Well. I've been a freelance writer for the last five years. I also teach at the community college. Business. I was born and raised here in Boulder. I have a wife, she's a lawyer. Her name's Shay. Sets her sights on big shot politicians, mostly. We have four kids. 4 to 14. That's basically it. These days."

"You sound like my dad."

Dan laughed raspily and unconvincingly.

"I'll be back," she said. And went toward the counter for her drink.

By the time that she returned, he had regrouped enough to ask a question.

"So, who is your hero?"

"Alex Honnold," she said, and began blushing. Cheeks like peaches.

"Who's that?" Dan asked.

"Are you freaking kidding me?" she nearly shrieked, peaches dropping. "I mean. *Seriously*? You said on the phone that you wrote about climbers!"

"Oh. Sorry. You must have misunderstood me. Probably bad connection. I said lemurs. Not climbers. That article made it into the *Times*, actually. My daughter watches your YouTube videos, and suggested that I should write an article about you, too. She also suggested the lemur article. That kid loves Zoboomafoo."

\*

It was Friday, 10:30 pm. Johnny walked alone into The Jackalope, hunched over. Wearing a cowboy hat and a tucked-in, buttoned shirt. Built like Yosemite's Half Dome. The place was mostly full. He ordered his drink and sat down, knees too tall to go under the table.

Guys snuck looks past their dates at Johnny as he watched the TV in the corner, where an old, rich, and fat man talked to the camera beside a former supermodel, his much younger wife. 'Governor Strider beats Forster in court,' the text read as the camera switched to a woman in a pantsuit, walking down a hallway, shaking her head.

"Damned socialists," Johnny muttered to himself.

He lived and worked on the plains, but drove his truck to the city at the foot of the Rockies on Fridays. For the past year or so, since he quit university and Northern's basketball team, his sister had been letting him crash on her couch until he headed back each Sunday evening. He could tell that staying with her wouldn't last much longer. Carson, her new boyfriend, didn't like 'loafers.'

The place was getting noisier. The guitar player on the stage was about to start. Johnny hadn't been to this bar before. It was getting harder to find new ones. After a drink, he put his hands together and looked at the bruises. Almost gone. It had gotten easy to tell which guys had something to prove, and someone who they wanted to prove it to. He always told his sister that he didn't start it. Which was usually the truth.

No one was playing pool yet, but Johnny had all night to wait and a week's worth to spend.

*

"So how did you lose the fingers," Dan said, more than a little sharply. Things had gotten testier since the lemur misunderstanding had been brought to light.

"Everest." Miyuki took a sip of her coffee before continuing. "The climb was alright. But not as rad as I had hoped. I was looking up at the asses of a small army of rich doctors and lawyers the whole time. That's not why I climb."

"Amazing," Dan said, scribbling notes. "Why do you climb?"

She looked off into space, thoughtful. As if she

had never considered the question before.

Finally, she said: "It's thrilling to find something big, set my sights, and beat it. Take it. Make it my own."

Then, she pulled out her phone and started texting. Or maybe just surfing the web, he wasn't sure.

"What did you think when you made it to the top? Of Everest, I mean."

Without looking up, she said: "Where's my glove?"

After a few moments, he understood.

So, he tried to lighten the mood: "Well, at least you didn't lose your texting digits."

That stopped her thumbs. She looked up from her phone, which erased his smile, then showed him what used to be her middle finger. And left.

*

Elliot's long, tan fingers effortlessly alternated between somber chords. He strummed slowly. A one-man show, he was tall and thin. And handsome, at least on a dark stage.

In a crooning, honest voice, he sang: "People

are like rivers, some rage, some fall, some placidly flow, all due to landscape, but nobody seems to know."

Basically no one listened to the words. At best, most people just listened to how he said them. He had come to accept that. Tonight, there were a lot of people not listening. The tables were all full. At least sixty people, who'd each paid a $5 cover charge to get in. Not a bad night. Enough to pay most of the bills, at least.

A small crowd had gathered at the little place for dancing below the stage. Mostly women in cowboy boots and tight blue jeans. A few men in cowboy and baseball hats stood by them, pretending to dance. Elliot opened his eyes as he stopped singing and kept strumming. Like a bear limping toward a barrel baited with old donuts, he couldn't help but to look down. Most of the girls were looking up at him. He knew where those eyes led. Never as good as Becca, his wife. And never again, he'd swore to himself. And to Becca.

He closed his eyes again and sang some more.

An abrupt crash caused Elliot to open his eyes and made him along with everyone else look toward the back of the room. Near-silence, just grunts. A couple fools were swinging fists and pool sticks. Something cracked loudly. Hopefully a pool stick, not an arm, Elliot thought. It looked like the biggest guy was about to go down. He was humongous.

"Easy, guys, easy," Elliot said, just before the manager asked him to stop playing. The break, at least, gave him a chance to take a few drinks, which made the playing easier.

After a few minutes he resumed performing and continued until the cops came, which interrupted his set for a bit. He'd never seen such an ordeal. By the time the ambulance had arrived, Elliot was done and heading out the door. Alone. And proud to be so.

To himself, he musically muttered: "I was small, then I grew, they got on top of me, just for the view."

Probably wouldn't be a song, he knew. Definitely wouldn't be running it by Becca, who had begun calling herself his co-writer.

\*

A woman around 40, wearing a turtleneck, sat alone with a latte at a high table in front of a laptop. Brunette. Tall and thin. Moccasins. Dark hair in a ponytail. Looking at the back of Dan's bald head.

When he stood, she said: "Excuse me, Dan? Dan Forster? I couldn't help but overhear your conversation. Are you the author of 'Learning from Lemurs,' in the *Times*?"

"Yes," he said, turning around and blushing almost as much as Miyuki had when Honnold was first mentioned. "That's me."

"I absolutely loved it! And the *Times*! I can only imagine. As an aspiring author myself, I'd *love* to pick your brain for a little while. And it's all about who you know, right? I'd love to know you. Would you mind?"

With her foot, she pushed the chair opposite from her, closest to him, away from the table. Dan felt truly big for the first time in over 20 years. No one had ever recognized his writing before. Not in person, at least.

"You probably get this all the time," she said.

"Every now and then."

He sat down, as she quickly closed her laptop.

"My name's Rebecca," she said liltingly, tilting her head slightly and smiling.

"Dan. So. If you liked 'Learning from Lemurs', then you'll really love 'In Her Shadow: A Husband's Struggle.' It's published. Just google it."

"Oh! Let me get a pen," she said, then began writing the name down. "I'll read it and let you know what I think. How should I contact you?"

He gave her his card.

"So," she said smiling, broadly. "What is your latest idea for a story?"

"Well. You won't tell anyone, will you?"

She leaned closer.

"Of course not."

*

"Whoa, buddy," Dan said listlessly as he walked into his wife's office, "You sure are tall. And ripped."

"Oh, come on in!" Shay said sarcastically from her desk. "Johnny, this is my husband, Dan. Dan, this is my client, Johnny. The police stud—I mean stun-gunned him to within an inch of his life. I just counted 43 burn marks on his back. We're going to make him a whole lot of money."

"That's the plan," Johnny said, as he put his shirt back on. And then he sat down in the leather chair in front of Shay's desk.

"We're almost done here, Dan," Shay said as she took notes on a legal pad.

Dan sat down by the window, to Johnny's right

and Shay's left.

"Why did they shock you so much?" Dan asked. "Did you deserve it?"

"Oh, don't mind him," Shay said before Johnny could respond. "Dan is just grumpy because a story that he was excited about got scooped. Some chick flirted with him and he told her about his idea. Emailed her an outline, even! And, she just published the story. About a mountain climber."

"No, Shay. The story wasn't about a mountain climber. That was another story that I won't be writing. But I guess that's beside the point."

"Johnny, let me go make a couple copies for you. I'll be right back."

After Shay left the room, it was quiet for several moments.

"So, what's your next story going to be?" Johnny asked sharply.

"Well, Johnny. To be honest, I'm not sure I've got another one in me."

"Sure you do," Johnny said, painfully shifting in his chair.

He looked at Dan for the first time; left eye still faintly bruised and fully unsettling.

"Maybe your next story is right in front of you. Seriously, man, what do you think your next story will be?"

Dan looked out the window at nothing in particular and thought about the offer sitting in front of him that would surely upset his wife.

"I think I'm going to have to ask my daughter. She's got some pretty good ideas, actually. And she's still small enough that she likes talking to me."

*

Elliot was sitting on the couch in his living room. He was wearing just his boxers and a trucker hat, watching birds at the feeder which were golden in the late-morning light. He held a white beer can, which rested on his right knee.

"Babe," Becca said, looking at him via the mirror in front of her as she finished applying make-up. "There is no easy way to say this. I have to go."

"What was that?"

Turning from the mirror, she took a few steps toward him.

"My story was just published in the *Times*. The

*Times!*"

"Yeah, I know it. That's why we celebrated last night."

"I can't keep this momentum going from Boulder. I've been here long enough."

Elliot held his face for a moment, three fingers on each eyelid. He knew she was serious.

"But you can write from anywhere," he managed to say. "There was a time, Becca, when a record label was interested in *me*. Remember that? Back when I was just beginning to be more than a man on a stage to you. And look at me now. What are you going to do when they don't think your next story is so great?"

"I guess I'll find out."

"Please, don't go. I've been good for over a year now."

"I know you have," Becca said, as she walked toward the door and from the closet took a suitcase that she'd packed while he was sleeping. "But to be brutally honest, I think I'd rather share a Randy Travis than have a Townes Van Zandt all to myself."

"Come on, don't you say that," Elliot said. And then took a long drink.

"Maybe you'll write a song about me leaving you."

"Don't be ridiculous. Seriously, Becca. This is not going to work out well for you. Next thing you know, you'll be broke in Denver without a plan."

"You're right, Elliot. I don't know how this will pan out. But right now, I can tell you that I'm moving out and I'm moving up."

She opened the door. The birds noisily scattered and the bright, warm light made her and the situation terribly clear. Then the door slammed and she was gone.

For a long time, Elliot sat there, stunned. They'd been married for nine years. Finally, he couldn't resist anymore. He grabbed the pencil and notebook from the coffee table in front of him. And then he wrote:

*Well, I made that Greensboro woman mine,*

*And like her husband then I'm left behind*

He stared at those lines for about 30 seconds. Then, he ripped the page out of the notebook, crumpled it, and threw it against the wall. And let it sit there for about two minutes, until he thought of another line.

"This is the one," he said, as he got up. He grabbed the balled paper from the corner, then began un-wadding and smoothing it. "This is the one that's gonna make it big."

*Laughing Gulls*

by

D.B.

They walked through the doors of the clean, newish bar and grill down by the ocean. A pleasant breeze met them first, followed by a smiling, older woman.

"Just two, today?"

"Yes," he said.

"Inside or out?"

He looked to his wife.

"Outside," she said.

"Let's see. Are there any open tables?" the greeter said to herself, looking at a laminated paper. "Lunch-time rush. Yes, one left."

All three of them walked by the bar, which was nearly full of people. Almost everyone, it seemed, was watching a game on a screen or elsewhere.

Most of the watchers were men wearing neatly-trimmed beards and Red Sox caps. Only one of the people at the bar didn't appear to be watching anything but, rather, seemed to be waiting. She, a young woman who looked to be Middle Eastern, sat alone with a cocktail glass in her hands while staring at the brick wall on the other side of the bar. Her right foot slowly danced. She wore a colorful, patterned skirt and dark, reddish-purple lipstick.

The attentive man walking behind his wife and the greeter slowly moved through the bar area, but he couldn't watch the people there for long. He'd been a 'people watcher' since he was a child. Soon he had walked through the garage-style doors which had been slid open and was outside, where he found an entirely new social environment. People were clumped at densely arranged tables, some under an umbrella, and some not. Children cried, parents scolded, old men gloated, and everyone seemed to be competing for the title of who could talk the loudest.

"Here you are," the greeter nearly yelled, pointing to a table under an umbrella. "Someone will be with you shortly."

The two sat down.

"They sure do pack us in tight out here," she said, beginning to look at the menu, settling into the cacophony of conversations. "Almost as tight as during the tram-ride here."

*Why even bother to look? We both know that you are going to get a garden salad, with Italian dressing and a side of fries. And a bottled water.*

"What are you hungry for, Mandy?"

She didn't hear. Or pretended not to.

*Not important. Don't push it. It really is very noisy out here.*

As he began looking at the menu, he noticed the waitress at the table behind his wife. He felt the familiar, spontaneous frenzy of flames spreading through his chest and belly. And the wanderings of his mind. He tried not to stare.

*My God. An angel. Those angles. Like a Puma.*

While she scribbled something on a pad, her tan face offered a little smile that revealed pure-white teeth. She bent down in her V-neck to point at the menu, said something, laughed, and walked away in jean shorts. Her long, dark braid flicked like a cat's tail.

 "What can I get started for you?" said a cheery voice. "Let's begin with drinks."

He looked up, from the Puma's path, to see their waitress.

*Dressed the same. Smiles the same. But twenty years and pounds more. Not as likely to make as much from tips, at least from guys. Isn't that sad? What a circus.*

"I'm still thinking about it," she said, without looking up from her menu.

"We'll need a few more minutes, please," he said. "I'll take a lemonade."

The Puma came back and he watched again. She balanced an ungodly amount of food on a platter. And skillfully laughed at whatever was said.

*Why does she have my attention? Because I'm like a damned dog. Which sees a steak dinner and drools, despite being well-fed. But I don't have to eat, or think about, what I don't want to. I can see what is not good for me.*

His wife put down her menu.

"Dave. Have you thought any more about names?"

He had not.

"Well," he said. "What about Anders?"

She thought a moment.

"I don't like it. People would think he is Swedish. Or something."

"Have you thought of any?"

"Liam. Robert. We'd call him Bobby, like my uncle. Or maybe Antonio."

"But wouldn't people think he was Italian if we called him Antonio?"

"I like Italian," she said, grinning a little. "And our first date was at Tony's Pizza. Might be appropriate."

*What a beautiful woman. Hazel eyes, curly bangs. And dimples. I need to remember to see them. I love that smile.*

"Could be appropriate," he agreed. "I'll give it some thought."

"Dave, I'm really glad that we bought a ranch-style house. Cassandra was right. It is *so* much easier to not have to mess with stairs, now that I'm growing."

She placed her hands on the little bump of her stomach.

"You did a great job finding our home," she continued. "I just love the style, that it's ranch."

Their waitress briskly returned from somewhere behind an umbrella. She placed the lemonade in front of Dave.

"Are we ready yet?"

"I'll have a garden salad," Mandy said. "With a small fry. And water. Bottled."

"What kind of dressing?"

"Ranch."

*Really, ranch? Not Italian? OK.*

"Alrighty. And you, sir?

"I'll take a cheeseburger. Ketchup and mustard. Pickles. Thank you."

The menus were taken away and Mandy began looking at her phone. Another chorus of grating and shrill laughs game from behind them where a group of older women sat in the sun.

"I'll be right back," Dave said. "Gotta use the restroom."

As he headed inside, the Puma was heading back to her section. 'Stacy,' her tag said in large, Sharpied letters drawn with sweeping curves. When she was a table away, he caught her sneaking a glance at him.

Almost frantically, she said, "have a nice day!" He thought he saw her blush as she hurried away, back towards Mandy.

*Josh would take advantage. He'd come back here later. Alone. But that's not for me. Never was or will be.*

Dave breathed in citrus-scented fragrance that he thought was from her as he headed to the men's room. Once inside, he looked at the mirror.

*She's right. I am still handsome. Despite my crooked nose. And the way that Mandy makes me dress, I look rich.*

He ran his fingers through his black, and a little gray, hair. Which was still somewhat thick.

*Being had by someone sure seems to make something more wanted by someone else. And sometimes I'm that something. So, I'm sure, is Mandy.*

He went over to the urinal, still meditating.

*What a sick species we are. Made to want what we don't have and to forget the value of what we do have.*

"Nooo-ohhhhh!" The scream came shrilly from the handicap stall. "Aaahhhhhhhh!"

Dave jumped so much that his stream almost hit the wall. As it dribbled to a stop, he looked over his right shoulder.

A toddler with a warrior-like scowl on his face emerged from beneath the handicap stall. One pudgy arm wrapped around the pole that held the stall up. Diaper around his ankles.

The door to the stall opened as Dave zipped up. A frazzled guy, with a hairline that was just beginning to recede, appeared. An ugly, brown-green stain zig-zagged across the bottom of his shirt.

"Sorry about that, man," he said, wrangling his son. "I'm still new to diaper changing."

The young father laughed.

*Am I ready for this?*

Dave headed back to Mandy.

"Are you OK?" she asked. "You look a little pale."

"I'm fine."

"Look at these colors. What do you like best for Antonio's room?"

She held her phone across the table for him to look at, elbow resting near the center. He saw panels of colors ranging from shades of blue to green.

"I like sky blue," she said.

He thought of the Puma's eyes. Of how they had sparkled light blue, before quickly looking away.

"I like blue, too. A light blue. I really like that."

*Terrible! Be stronger than that. Pretty girls, with their smiles and words, are just Nature's flowers. Meant to use stupid and charming bees. Which I won't be. Mandy is enough for me.*

He looked at his beautiful wife, as she intently scrolled through colors.

"Mandy, I want you to know that I love you. You are all I need."

Bewilderedly, for a moment, she looked at him.

"I know. I love you too."

She went back to focusing on her phone.

"Are we still planning on watching a movie with Josh and Cassie tomorrow?" he asked.

"As far as I know."

*Polygamists like them sure are noisy. They say monogamy isn't Natural. But the internet says birds do it, too. Splitting up love and attention leaves less for each person, or bird, right? Makes bonds less strong. And how can jealousy be—*

"What, honey?" he asked.

"Those damned sea gulls won't shut up!"

*Just like the polygamists.*

She looked somewhat angrily at the sky. Four were screaming and chasing another. The one being chased held a shimmering little fish in its bill and had a black head that, appropriately, looked like a thief's mask.

"Well, I guess that I get hangry, too," Mandy said. "It is like they would prefer that no one eat if they aren't eating."

She laughed and put down her phone.

"Do you think that they are happy together? Josh and Cassandra?" she asked. "You know. With their arrangement."

"Um. I think that—"

"Here you are, folks!"

Their waitress placed the cheeseburger, which

looked lonely in its basket, in front of him. Then the salad, fries, and water in front of her.

"Looks great, thanks," he said.

Just after their waitress walked away, a nearby older woman wearing a red wig that shined brightly in the sun screeched: "I need another margarita!"

Their waitress nodded and cheerily said: "I'm on it."

*That must get so old.*

Dave began eating. After a few bites, he looked over at Mandy. She was scowling. And looking at her salad like the family of a victim looks at a murderer in a courtroom.

"Dave. Look."

She gestured at her salad. Thick white lines of ranch dressing zig-zagged across the lettuce and tomatoes.

"Is there something wrong?"

"The f*cking ranch dressing, Dave. They screwed up my order."

"Well." He considered his words carefully. "Do you think that you might have asked for ranch on accident?"

Sharply, she said: "Why do you always defend *them*, Dave? And not me. Remember what Dr. Crenshaw says. We are a team and should act like it. Sometimes you need to knock the other guy down."

*Maybe Crenshaw wants me to get into a fight so we have to keep coming to see him. And funding his office renovation.*

"I'll flag down the waitress," he said.

"No. It's fine."

She began moving around lettuce with her fork and he raised his hand for their waitress to see.

"I said it's fine, Dave."

She commenced shoveling salad in, angrily. And he put his hand down.

*She has a universe inside of her, too. Let it be. We're all made crazy. And stay that way until we do something about it.*

He looked at the Puma again, then at the couple that she was serving.

"How are y'all doing today?" he heard her say, sweetly.

The couple was about the same age as him and

Mandy. They sat in chairs right next to each other, her arms around one of his as they began looking at a single menu.

*They look happy. Strong, together. A closer look and I'd see the cracks. We've looked closely, with Crenshaw's help. And are stronger than we might think after looking at others from a distance.*

He took another couple bites.

*I need to write that one down.*

He pulled his phone out of his pocket and began opening the 'notes' app.

"Dave, can we just focus on our food. For once. Put it away, please."

After a moment of hesitation, and a deep breath, he did.

As he finished his burger, he looked inside at the bar, where he could just barely see the young Middle Eastern woman who had been sitting alone. A man with a beard and a baseball cap, who had been watching television further down the bar, now sat by her.

*Let them be flowers. Let them be bees. I never enjoyed the buzzing.*

"How was everything today?" their waitress

asked, after handing a margarita to the red-wigged woman.

"Everything was great, thanks," Mandy said.

"Will you be having any desserts on this fine afternoon?" she asked.

"No. Check, please," Dave and Mandy said simultaneously.

"OK, I'll be right back."

"Want to pick up that paint on our way home?"

Mandy put a finger to her lips, thoughtfully, then smiled broadly.

"Yes, I think so."

"Here you are, folks," their waitress said as she left the check.

*$22. Thirty should do it. A bonus for the tips she loses due to experience. And for all those crazies she has to deal with.*

Dave put down a twenty and a ten, then stood. Mandy stood too.

"Don't you think that your tip is a bit much? She did mess up my order."

"I think it's fine, honey. Maybe she is having a

bad day and could use the money to cheer herself up. Let's go get some paint."

Mandy looked at him and shook her head.

"Dave, Dave, Dave," she said, almost lovingly. "Let's not let Antonio see you throw our money away like this."

On their way out, as they left the noisy tables outside and entered the cool barroom, he grabbed her hand when he smelled citrus-scented perfume and didn't look around to see who was looking at him.

Dave and Mandy both smiled as the gulls argued overhead.

What was left of a small fish dropped from the sky. It spiraled as it fell, and all five of the birds swooped after it. But they thwarted each other's efforts. And the shiny little morsel fell squarely into the half-full glass of a loudly laughing woman. She didn't notice the *ker-plunk* because at that very moment she was reaching for her hair as it threatened again to fly away. But she caught it and, satisfied, took another big gulp.

"Squawk, squawk!" she cried, looking up. "I hate birds."

Everyone flew away frustrated. Cackling. Plotting. And hungry.

There was thirst, too: "Excuse me, miss. Excuse me! Another margarita! With a little less *salt* this time."

*Bye Bye*

by

J.B.

My boss calls me on the phone and tells me to come to his office with a queer and foul look on his face. The face he uses that looks like how a dead raccoon smells. It's not like I've never seen it before, we used to imitate it in the break room. Me, Kevin from sales and Samir of accounting. But not as of late. Kevin was fired and Samir deported back to... you know it's funny, seven years' worth of water cooler conversation and I never did ask Samir his home's whereabouts. It's just funny.

I'd feel worse about it if it weren't for the screaming baby in the elevator. Doesn't the thing know I'm stressed enough as it is? Somebody give that baby some candy I can steal. The mother smiles sheepishly at me with that, ah-shucks, kids-am-i-right? facial tick. I could roundhouse her right now. Rumor has it the elevator cam. is down.

At the 13th floor, the elevator blips and dings to a halt. I depart and immediately go limp in my right, far superior leg. I make my way to the bathroom for a much-needed vomital exercise. Jesus Christ, I need to lay off the egg salad. My leg returns along with my courage, not quite what it used to be, but I'm still technically a successful white male so, f*ck it right? I skip the bathroom and head to my boss's office.

Knock knock.

No reply. The plant to the left sways. You heard that right?

Knock knock.

 "Come in!"

My butt acts as a heat seeking missile for the leather-plated bitch seat. Mr. Foster takes maybe two, maybe three meetings a day in his office, and yet his guest chairs are better than the rest of the office's combined. Just an observation.

"Thanks for having me Mr. Foster! I love what

you've done with the place. Are those new curtains?"

I feel as if I am a deer in the hunt. Best keep my offerings ripe.

Mr. Foster overrides and proceeds: "Do you know why I called you in here, Dixon?"

I stiffen up like an erection and stifle a mid-day burp.

"No sir, does it have anything to do with those quarterlies? Because I could have sworn I really knocked them out of the park."

My tzar strokes his chin and resolves to chatter.

"I bought those curtains in Taiwan. My intent was the family room. Back home you see. Nancy didn't take to them. She couldn't appreciate their, oh their," he bobs his head back and forth while juggling for an answer, playing with his company pen, "their pompous attitude."

Then nothing. It's my turn.

"I really like them sir, I absolutely adore pompous attitude. I mean for gosh shakes sir, it's my middle name!"

I laugh at my dumb joke, just as I did with every dumb girl dumb enough to let me in.

Nothin. It's his turn, right? A cricket orgasms. I forego conversation etiquette, full steam ahead.

"It's funny because, I mean that's not a middle name sir. And anyways, I mean, who in their right mind gives a child two middle names?"

Foster smiles. Hallelujah there really is a God.

"That's a mighty keen sense of humor you got there Dixon. Unfortunately for you, I didn't bring you in here for sh*ts and giggles. Sh*ts and giggles are for employees who conform. Comply. Step in line like a goddamn Nazi on his way to an infant's execution. You get what I'm saying, Mr. Middle Name? I bought you to play dutiful employee in this system, *my system*. You think I pay you but in fact it is *you* paying *me*. Your life, from your daddy long leg stature all the way up to your pickled ears. Your ass is mine Dixon! So let me ask you once and once only, why on God's green earth are you wearing a bandana, in my office!"

It is true. I've been wearing a pink bandana on my head for two weeks now. My dear sister was recently diagnosed.

"I'm so sorry sir, it's so dumb I didn't think—"

"You're goddamn right you didn't think! Now, Dixon I like you. Your work is modest. You stay in your lane and we share a birthday. I appreciate you sharing in my embarrassment

34

on the 5th of every 12th month, with that pathetic song and dismal confetti." He shutters. "Now if you can cease with the abysmal attire we are square. Do I make myself clear Dixon?"

"Yes sir."

I rise as if dynamite is set to erupt any minute underneath the chair's leathery goodness. But before I can grasp the door's slender handle, he offers one final touch.

"Oh, and Dixon. Step out of line again and I'll ship you off to wherever the f*ck that Samir f*ck landed. Bye bye."

*Gas Lights*

by

O.B.

Coldness never bothered Mario at first, but it
might have killed him with its creeping,
hypnotic persistence. Warmth, on the other
hand, tended to skip right over the pleasant,
rosy sensations of toasty milk and soft butter
for Mario Valesquez, and go right into a
discomforting burn. A tolerance for
temperatures in excess was one reason that for
the last twenty-two years Mario had enjoyed
his career—which, unfortunately, had ended
recently. There was nothing that ensured
discomfort like jumping out of helicopters into
desert, arctic, or urban theme parks. Not even a
bad case of gas in a bustling hallway.
Discomfort made Mario feel alive, but it would

be hard to justify experiencing it now.

Mario knew enough about the risks of exposure to be ashamed that he had let his hands get frostbitten. Despite the late summer season, hypothermia was a risk whenever a person was wet and the ambient temperature dropped below 75°. Lui, the psych nurse who came by with a deck of cards twice a day to check in and play a round of Five Hundred, had landed a good rapport with Mario. He reminded Mario to feel guilty about the list of conditions he was admitted with, if he must, but not ashamed.

"Save the shame for men less handsome than you," Lui had said, a shameless flirt. Mario was going to miss him.

Well, miss him in the way a second grader misses their schoolteacher who looks the other way when they wipe a booger under their desk. Wholesome yet distant enough that you can take their advice without feeling bad about those times when you pointedly don't take their advice.

That's probably what Mario found irritating when he looked at the Band-Aids on his knuckles; he hadn't taken his own advice about proper cold weather care. Fuzzy bits of fiber stuck in a thin layer at the periphery of his bandages. A good sign that the damage site shrank in the past week, but also reminders of the frost blisters Mario won during a course he had sat on a waiting list to take. Frost blisters. As an EMT, the worst Mario had been hurt was to break his foot from landing on it wrong. Mario peeled fuzz from the adhesive with distracted pathos.

A woman's voice said: "Mr. Valesquez?"

"Hmm?"

"Call for you. Christine Velasquez is on your line."

"Oh," Mario said.

"The one on the right, remember? The left rejects the waiting line."

"Oops."

"It's alright, it'll default to the nurse's station. It'll flash in a minute and that's your wife. Pick up and push the one on the right to accept the line. Okay? The one on the right."

"Got it, thank you."

Mario answered, acutely aware of the same nurse hovering outside the door to make sure he did. Lui had probably made some note about encouraging Mario's communication with his wife. What a sh*t.

"Hey Chris, thanks for calling."

"Paige, the nurse, said you're getting discharged today. Thought we could go to Top Indian Palace to celebrate. How are you feeling? Hands better?"

*She's nervous. Guess I would be too if she had rejected my call.*

"So they say, heh, TIP sounds nice but I'm not sure I'll be home in time for fancy dinner out. Still planning to meet Coop at West Joint after they let me go."

Mario settled in for a talking to.

"Wait. Coop? Cooper Ewing? That's the friend you're driving all the way to Leadville to see?"

"Thought I might."

"Honey, Coop is a dickhead. I thought we talked about his—"

"He paid for my course."

"What?"

"In the exit interview, before they put me on the bus with the other guys, Mr. Diarrhea and the other guy and the one with the punctured lung. Yea, turns out the receipt of payment comes with the summary packet. Dr. Ewing, it says right there, 'paid in full.'"

"Is that why he wants to see you, to guilt trip you about it?"

"I don—"

"What's his angle?"

"Babe, don't be like that, he was probably just trying to be nice. He has kind of been aloof since Mary left. I'm glad to hear from him again."

"Don't go, honey. Every time you come back from 'catching up,' you're a mess..."

"We were texting. And, at first, I felt just like you do. Which I told him. But he's sure it's just me making mountains out of moles."

"It's mole hills, and that's classic Coop. I don't want you to go. Come home and let's go to TIP."

"Chris, I don't think it'll take that long."

"OK, if that's where you want to be."

"I don't want to not be home with you."

"What do you want, Mario?"

Mario crumpled a corner of his course summary.

"I want to stay married to you..."

That made Chris laugh.

"...and, I also want to see if I can catch up with Coop. Seems like he's doing much better."

Chris didn't laugh a second time.

"Babe, I promise I won't drink. What's the harm?"

"Mario, if I was even a little worried that you'd lie to me about drinking, I wouldn't have called and admitted to them that I'm your spouse."

The tension weighed heavily on the line, enough to soften Chris into letting up.

"Just call me when you decide what to do?" she said. "I miss my Candyman."

After twelve years, Mario still felt a teenage rush under his skin when Chris used his bedroom name in public. Even a public phone. Rubbing his right hand through his fresh haircut, Mario tried for a clean exit.

"Oh, Chris, you make it hard to be a good friend."

"Takes a good friend to be a good friend, Mario. Just call me when you're an hour out, okay?"

"Yea, I'll call you when I'm almost home."

"Okay. Be safe. I hope not all of you is frost bitten."

"I try not to expose tender parts of myself to the cold, woman."

They both hung up without saying good-bye. Mario tried not to think about checking to see if Cooper had already canceled his invitation or not. He applied a dab of prescription ointment to the raw patch on his nose, quelling the healing itch, for the moment.

Pages, stapled neatly in their upper left corner, riffled under Mario's peeling finger pads. He had time to review his scores again while waiting for someone to bring his bags and effects (they had only brought him a change of clothes from his locker). They'd also need to provide directions to the carpool lot where his heirloom Chevrolet awaited. He'd opted to pay for a ride-share to bring his car over from Stone Age Survival, Inc.'s extended-stay lot. Presently, it was somewhere in the extended parking zone on the main hospital's south wing. Once again, Mario read through the comments and scores:

> Wilderness First Responder, Score: 94%

Primitive Living Intensive, Score: 88%

Advanced Navigator (Team Trial),
Score: 78%

Final Score: 86%

Comments: Participant displayed above-average intuition and morale. Background education (Earth Knack LLC) and career experience appreciated; special thanks for soap making and quality food preparation insight was noted by trial teammates, Aaron Barb and Michele Gutierrez. "Unparalleled sportsmanship" recognized by Mr. Barb. All three listed participants reported exhaustion and fatigue-related illness upon completion of Advanced Navigator Team Trial. Mr. Velasquez was the only one from his team dispensed to receive treatment.

Sustained injuries to hands, knees, and facial tissues from frostbite. Reported symptoms emerged on day 38. Frostbite sustained and apparent upon collection (ahead of deadline!) at pick-up site on day 39. Injury to muscle and/or skeletal function sustained from aggravating previous injury (see Service Record for details; Service ID 9222815382). Full exit course interview conducted before participant officially completed the program on day 41. Transferred with other injury cases to West Holt Memorial Hospital on day 41.

<u>Highly recommended for Instructor-in-Training Course</u>, on caveat that <u>involvement be limited</u> to classroom demonstrations or site walk-through prep.

Mario refolded the packet along its corrugations. The creases were darkening from use, as he had read it almost every other hour for the past six days. The course summary had become his favorite reading material right up until that last sentence, which always tempted Mario to tear it off.

He returned to peeling fuzz from Band-Aid residue and waited for the next person in scrubs to breeze through and let him sign the discharge forms.

\*

Dr. Knuddsen-Lee leaned back, readjusted paperwork, chose a pen (black ink rather than red), and between sips from a can of carbonated water commenced Mario's discharge check-up. Mario sat up on the edge of the hospital bed to display his eagerness to get going. When he stood up, Dr. Knuddsen-Lee asked him to sit back down. The admitting physician was out, so Mario was left in her hands.

"It says here that you experienced some moderate-to-severe hallucinations prior to coming in. Can you tell me about that?"

The doctor took a silent sip from the tinkling can, pen at-the-ready.

"What about it?"

Mario hadn't meant to be sharp, but Lui asked him about how he was, regarding that specificity, twice daily since he was admitted. It was a tiring topic to rehash for yet another round of psych evaluations. His answers to Lui had become progressively more open and less programmed. This doctor, however, emanated an aura of no-nonsense.

Mario absently scratched a scab under his canvas pant leg.

"When did you start experiencing hallucinations?"

"Think about two days out."

"From the start of the training period?"

Concerned note taking ensued.

"Out from the finish line," Mario corrected.

It wasn't the doctor's questions that conveyed concern. Rather, Mario knew the more notes that were taken directly corresponded to the amount of double and triple-checking Dr. Knuddsen-Lee would be doing on his medications list, prior incident records, and whatever else paperwork now followed him through the ether of civilian record keeping. Mario was mellow at baseline and knew discharge interviews are a crucial time to channel mellowness. But there were *a lot* of notes being taken. Mario wiggled to readjust himself with forced nonchalance.

"There was maybe... eighteen or twenty miles left in the river nav. portion and me and the other two guys were just sleep deprived."

He wiggled again under the patient silence that Dr. Knuddsen-Lee offered, inviting him to continue.

"We alternated paddling," Mario offered. As if that answered the unspoken question.

"And the paddling, that was the source of the," the doctor glanced back down at her shielded notes, "the hallucinations? Or the severe exhaustion and Stage II hypothermia? Or both?"

"No, I mean, yes. Weird things happen in the field after so many hours without sleep or rest. You just start to go a little wobbly with your motor skills or your vision gets spotty. It's one of the reasons we have mandatory relief crews for medivac scheduling—"

"Yes, that seems like a good idea for such demanding work."

"Anyway," Mario powered on, "we were in teams of three for the last chunk of it. Michele and Aaron were the other two," *like she cares*, "and the navigation course had us ending on a river."

The doctor took another sip of carbonated water, and waited.

"We got into some sh*t with one canoe and to make up time we paddled the last few days straight in the other. We even finished the course in record time—yea, anyway—between the 60-odd hours without sleep and the two-hour stints of hard pushing upriver, I started to see colored, 3D shapes and things in the trees along the bank. Then, ya know, they started to get sharper and brighter and move around and—"

"That's hallucinating," Dr. Knuddsen-lee finished for him.

"Mhm. They looked like old oil or gas lamps flickering and sputtering. Aaron saw them too," Mario added, defensively. "After I brought it up. We were two days out, and we all knew we were getting fried, but we just kept paddling."

Mario wasn't fidgeting anymore. A light sweat misted his chest and armpits as he continued to stumble through his answers. Not because narrating the extremes of the course was stressful, but because the doctor kept making notes for several second intervals when Mario would stop talking for any length of time.

He could only sit and actively ignore the pink fluid seeping out from one Band-Aid and into the fabric covering one knee as he watched Dr. Knuddsen-Lee take notes. Then, out of nowhere, the railroad yard popped into his head. The railroad yard Cooper brought him to the day after he'd asked Coop not to jerk off in the family bathroom. Mario had to ask, because his parents didn't want Coop to come over anymore if he was going to spend half of his time in the bathroom. Mario agreed to say something to his friend, but only because he caught second-hand embarrassment from the smell Coop left behind. Mario had been Catholic enough to hide his own business.

He had thought Coop would get angry or embarrassed that day, they'd only been 13 and 12, but Coop just went quiet for a beat before laughing the rest of the time they played Mario Kart. The weekend after that, he'd showed Mario the abandoned railroad depot with the large limestone blocks that hid their new hideout from the road.

"Do you need a change?"

Someone was touching Mario's knee. It was Dr. Knuddsen-Lee. No, he realized, her hand wasn't touching his knee but cautiously halting his own hand from touching his own knee.

"We could all use a little change," Mario said, trying to sing the lyrics but sounding a hair too vacant to land his desired effect.

"Your wraps," the doctor said as she rubbed one of Mario's Band-Aided knuckles with agitating gentleness, "do you need them to be changed before you go? If they're itchy, they probably do need to be swapped out."

"That'd be great, thanks."

More scratching onto the form.

"And what makes a person want to do something so extreme?"

Cavernous brown irises bored into Mario for the first time since the doctor swiveled the plastic seat to face him. Mario didn't move to de-fuzz the adhesive on his hand. The resultant tickle gnawed at him.

"Canoe to the finish line?" he asked.

"Canoe until you hallucinated streetlights."

"They weren't streetlights, I said lamps," Mario spat. "Like old gas ones that used to suffocate people in their homes."

Mario couldn't place why the distinction mattered, but it did. They'd existed in his mind, after all, so the details were important for a psych evaluation.

Dr. Knuddsen-Lee studied him before reframing the question: "What made you want to push so hard that you landed here for almost a week?"

"You're asking about trauma history, and I already cleared that up with Lui. Not all of us are messed up because of what we do. It's sh*tty to constantly tell us that, and I'm not a vet. the way you think. I was an EMT and never even saw enemy fire..."

He saw what combat did to people, though, and in the farthest recesses of his conscience Mario knew all those things he'd experienced had consequences. Bad things happened. Sometimes those bad things can be sewn back up, defibrillated, and—in the case of Stage II hypothermia—the patient can come back to life if thermal pads are applied in time.

"...I took all the stateside education classes and passed group without being diagnosed with anything more than general anxiety. And only when people push me."

Mario swallowed the spit pooling in his cheeks, before continuing.

"So, no, Dr. Hard Ass, I took the course because I like being outside and have been doing this sh*t since I was a Cub Scout. I'll have you know, I learned basket weaving good enough to sell them as a fundraiser for my Eagle Award."

Mario's hands were now clean of excess Band-Aid adhesive. He crossed them authoritatively over his dewy chest. Dr. Knuddsen-Lee shaded her eyes from the window's glare. She didn't write anything down.

"What will you do with the rest of your day, Mr. Velasquez?"

"There's not a whole lot of day left. Anyway, I gotta see a friend in Leadville before I get home."

"An old military buddy is going to ask you to delay you from seeing your spouse after the hospital?"

"No, he's not ex-military. He's a doctor friend, err, he became a doctor. We go way back, but no, Cooper never needed help paying for college." Embarrassed, Mario tried to recover his point, "He secretly paid for the training, actually. I think that calls for a beer, afterwards."

The doctor checked Mario's file on her aluminum clipboard.

"You don't drink."

Mario briefly considered asking if he should strip back to his skivvies, what with all these needling questions, but said nothing.

"Why did your friend pay for your course, do you think?"

Mario laughed inwardly at the strange avenue of empathy this acknowledgment cracked open between them.

"I don't know why he did it," he said. "We haven't seen each other in a couple years."

Mario left his arms crossed, his hesitation at seeing Coop in the first place falling to the back of his mind.

"Coop probably saw me share the course on Facebook and knew I couldn't afford it right now. He's a smart guy."

Dr. Knuddesen-Lee did not blink.

"Sounds like a very smart guy." One short scribble and the doctor crossed her own arms where she sat. "Seems a bit controlling, paying for something for someone you haven't seen in years. And also a bit harmful, considering it landed you in the hospital."

"Sure, but I didn't say we don't ever talk. Coop just shows up when he wants to."

Again she checked the clipboard and made a note.

"Looks like your wife called twice each day while you were here."

"She's like that."

"You only accepted four of her calls."

"We have our sh*t like everyone else."

The doctor moved the pen but it didn't make it to the form. In the brief time Mario watched Dr. Knuddsen-Lee do this, he floated back to their split-level on East 190th Street.

Chris had surprised him with a workshop she built into the back end of their garage, the week he came back from his final deployment. She even stocked it with second-hand equipment for sharpening blades. Mario's plan to make money after the service was to be a tool sharpener for small farms and barbers, at least until he decided whether to use his GI credits.

"Everything from chainsaws to a chef's arsenal could be sharpened right here," she had said brightly, all laugh lines and wild hair.

Mario remembered how he had acknowledged his wife's thoughtfulness by pointing out the lack of ventilation. Then, by explaining how the workshop reduced free space in their garage by nearly a third. He thought she was going to throw her usual argumentative attitude for being ungrateful, but Chris hadn't done anything. Not that day or any time before Mario left for the six-week (turned seven) survival course. In retribution for her lack of anger, Mario had ignored her calls and only fed her the baseline details about his admitted conditions. Ironically, Mario hoped the iceberg that had built up between them since then would melt on its own once he got back. Their phone conversation today had kindled that wee flame of hope.

Coop would understand that sort of thing. Dr. Cooper Ewing was a self-proclaimed Master of The Game, who—whenever he was visible in Mario's life—possessed a rare objectivity when it came to interpersonal quarrels.

Mario returned to the present to find Dr. Knuddsen-Lee standing, with no indication that Mario should sign something. A pleasant handshake and a warm, "I hope I never see you again, Mr. Valesquez," capped off the doctor's discharge. Dr. Knuddsen-Lee peeled out of the room, clipboard in hand.

Maybe it was the residual effects of his prednisone regime making him feel things he hadn't in a while, or the surprise at his own defensiveness about Coop's thoughtful gesture, but Mario decided to cast aside his doubts and meet up with Coop at West Joint. He only needed to gas up the car, noting the quarter tank left from being driven to the hospital, and he could make the time Coop set within an hour or so. Maybe sooner. Mario was unsure where this sense of urgency to meet Coop on his terms came from but it did not ring of friendly warmth. He loaded his single duffle bag into the back seat and slammed the door with unnecessary force. The car rocked a bit when he did. *Good*, thought Mario, *at least I can affect the car, the gas, the speed*, and went on to name other superfluous items empowering him in that moment.

Picking up 20, heading north out of Neligh, Mario waited for a stoplight to text Coop his ETA.

Mario had not expected Coop to pop into his personal musings as much as he had lately. Especially during the strenuous portions of the survival course. Which was curious, because Coop liked to remind Mario of how independent they both were and why that made their friendship 'one for the ages.' And it seemed like the more Mario got on with Aaron

Barb, the more Coop popped up, too.

\*

Four hours later, Mario pulled up the stubborn parking brake of his '81 Chevy, stepped onto the gritty grey concrete of his and Chris's split-level house, and stretched his back before unloading the bag with his toothbrush. The living room lights were out. Mario got out his cell to see if she was still up. If not, he would have to haul everything in through the back door. Chris picked up on the third ring.

"Hi, Christine Velasquez, here."

Her voice came through in tones of orange and yellow. Mario brushed one scabby knee nervously.

"Don't you ever check the ID before picking up?"

He punched the four-digit code into the keypad and turned from the obnoxious grinding of the garage door, phone to ear.

"Oh, honey," she yawned, "you know that crap is for people with time on their hands."

"Speaking of hands," Mario turned sideways to scoot by the sedan, "I think mine will need a bit of wifely TLC."

Chris opened the interior door while Mario's hand was still on the knob. They hung up in unison.

"Didn't think you'd be back until after ten."

"Still up for Indian?" he asked.

"The left-overs are waiting for you, bottom shelf."

Mario sped toward the kitchen, slapping a chapped-lip kiss on his wife's temple as he brushed passed.

"What did Coop have to say?"

"Not a whole lot. You know Coop."

Mario didn't turn from the refrigerator until he had a spoonful of saag in his mouth.

"Unfortunately," Chris said, reminding Mario just how terrifying his wife could be when offended.

He swallowed, put his bowl in the microwave, and slammed the door.

"I can give you details tomorrow, if you want."

She looked surprised and then irate.

"You sorted things out then?"

Definitely irate.

"Sure did," Mario lied, unleashing a playful wink on her, winning him a dazzling smile.

"Oh yea? Sounds fruitful. Use a bigger bowl! You just dribbled rice all over the tile."

"Ouch. Pffft."

Mario spat Indian food into the sink, having spooned a million-degree bite into his mouth without noticing the steam billowing off it.

"Well, I can see that you're in a good mood," Chris said, easing closer to him, her evening beer already half gone.

She poured him a glass of pomegranate-apple juice. He took it and they comically toasted to his instructor's positive feedback. Mario slid his non-Indian-food-shoveling arm around Chris's waist and brought her into a half hug.

"Sure am in a good mood," he said, grinning devilishly. "I just burned for you the whole drive home."

At Chris's insistence, Mario recounted the last seven weeks for her, until, his survival stories told, she called him Candyman.

*

Mario got up in the middle of the night and padded softly to the kitchen. As something to do until he felt tired again, he collected spilt rice and wiped up smeared bits of wayward garlic from the counter bar, the ancient carpet, and (amazingly) from a living room window. Mario knew he would need time to digest what had happened at West Joint before he elaborated more than he already had to Chris, who knew he was upset about the whole situation.

Mario reapplied Band-Aids to his cracked blisters, rubbed some Tiger Balm into his ankles, and popped one of the PRN anxiety meds Dr. Knuddsen-Lee had added to his discharge pharmacy order. Finally, Mario poured some juice and digested a smidge before sneaking back into bed. Where he thought again about what had happened at West Joint.

*

He had found Coop already inside, looking sharp as ever, waiting at a standing table. They moved to a booth when Mario admitted he was too sore to stand for long stints. He would have liked to leave his gloves on, to disguise the frostbite, but decided not to. Coop, though, didn't mock him for either obvious limitation. Forty-three minutes into their catching-up,

Mario opened a conversational door. But, instead of allowing their discussion of how great Asian food was to naturally branch to other topics, Coop jarringly asked about Mario's wife.

"Ah, yes, how is Prissy Chrissy?" Coop asked and smiled, casually.

Mario felt his neck tweak.

"She never goes by 'Chrissy,'" Mario said, voice pinching to match his expression. "Why did you say that?"

Mario straightened his posture as he awaited a response.

"Didn't mean anything by it, man, just interested in your life." Coop drank lazily. "Like, remember that time you called me in tears about divorcing her? Just showing support for a friend," Coop said before drinking again, and chortling. "Don't be so sensitive!"

Mario chose his words tenderly while playing with the ice in his tall glass.

"Coop, I don't think I'm all that sensitive. And Christine never went by a nickname other than Chris."

Neither spoke for half a minute, and that suited Mario fine. He stirred syrup with his plastic straw until it dissolved entirely into his drink. When the silence went on too long, Mario tossed his friend a bone.

"Actually, ya know, we did almost get divorced—two separate times!—but that was all within the first five years. We've been solid since all that."

"Ok, whatever you say, Mars Bar."

"What *is* that?"

"What is what?"

"That thing you do where nothing ever seems to affect you? I call you a handful of years ago, afraid my wife is sleeping around, and you bring that up now? After dropping some three grand on a survival course for me? Without even asking me? I got frostbite."

"Well, that's your own fault, sounds like nobody else got frostbite. And I don't know why you're mad, I wanted to do something nice for a friend and so I did. I have the money, so I tried to help. You're blowing one stupid remark way out of context. Let's talk about something else. You're always so paranoid. Relax. How was it, smoking venison and mapping the stars?"

Mario threw a tactical glare over his left shoulder. A few yuppies at the copper-topped bar were sipping liquor from sweating glassware garnished with curling citrus peals. A gaggle of old men, apparently retirees, were playing cards adjacent. Almost no were women floating about. Mario felt himself searching to find whoever it was that Coop was trying to impress.

He looked again into the face of his old buddy, and felt a chill. It gave him gooseflesh, hinting at what might lay at the crux of Coop's behavior. A tiny awareness sputtered to life like an old timey gas lamp inside his memory. Hundreds of arctic moments veined together like ice on the inside of his old Chevy's windshield. Suddenly Mario could see the closure that some part of him, deep inside, had thought he might be able to get by catching up with Coop.

"Remember that day at the depot when you accidentally grabbed my dick, when we were kids?"

Mario let the words fall to the floor like dead flies caught in a sub-zero gust.

"Of course I do," Coop flashed his perfect, white teeth between deep drafts of his beer, "but, you know, boys will be boys. Kids swap experimental blow jobs as a matter of self-discovery."

And there it was. When he saw the look on

Mario's face, Cooper poured placations out like ambrosia for the gods. The feel of sitting bare-assed on a sheltered block of frigid limestone momentarily swarmed Mario's senses.

Suddenly, Mario sucked down the remainder of his iced tea, stood up, strode to the bar, and paid for his and Dr. Ewing's libations.

Cooper's alarm at Mario's refusal to play his game sprinted across his face. And then he looked as surprised as a master woodworker who sees his smoothly-sanded hunk of oak unexpectedly fall off the lathe.

"I shouldn't have just sent in the money like that, I was trying to be discreet," Cooper said, directing his apology away from the critical issue.

"Good-bye, Coop," Mario said, cordially.

Zipping up his jacket, Mario pocketed his wallet, left a tip that was more than the tab, and headed for the breezeway of the West Joint.

"I know. I'm sorry," Cooper said in his 'this is all a stupid joke' voice.

The thick frost protecting Mario's heart all these years didn't just thaw. It altogether evaporated. Mario knew that Cooper's apology was bait, and he was much too big a fish to stay on one of Cooper Ewing's hooks anymore.

Hands shaking, Mario had Cooper's contacts blocked on all his accounts before even starting up the Chevy.

Not long into his drive, Mario turned off the air conditioner and imbibed the moisture-laden air in thick, satisfied gulps. He was struck by how coldness never bothered him at first, but he knew that it had almost killed him with that creeping, persistent lack of warmth.

*Crowfoot*

by

D.B.

Like it was Jesus she was talking about, or maybe Bono, Marybeth the mail carrier youthfully shrieked:

"Everybody, look. Here *he* comes!"

And everyone—literally all the people who lived in or near the remote village—looked down in the valley toward the setting sun and squinted. Sure enough, Marybeth was right. In the distance they could just make out the train, shimmering like an anchovy as it crossed the soggy, golden plains.

Alice Fairbanks, the mayor, looked like a ray of sunshine gracing the overcast evening in her bright-yellow poncho. A sturdy woman, her wavy hair was raven-black except for the gray streak that she had fastened behind her left ear. She grabbed her red megaphone—which had a very large horn—and into it energetically chimed, her breath just visible in the cool October air:

"Alright, folks. This is the moment that we've all been waiting for. President Remington will be passing through the great village of Crowfoot in about three minutes. Get your flags ready!"

There was a buzz of excitement in the usually-empty, half-asphalt and half-grass, quarter-acre lot between the railroad tracks and the general store. Ranchers made up about half of the group and most of them stood on their tailgates, careful not to slip in the light rain. People sitting in lawn chairs got up and looked down into the valley. The portable folks sat on the shoulders of the sturdy ones. The spry ones jumped up and down. The ones who could whistle whistled. Only the two Secret Servicemen in black suits didn't look particularly interested. The one with a buzzcut and thick-framed, dark glasses stood with his hands on his hips; the one that was bald with the physique of a body-builder was looking at his watch, while compressing and releasing an empty water bottle. Everyone else waved a little American flag, which Alice had given them. 'Vote Remington' signs with a couple pistols on them, from last year's election, also decorated the for-a-moment-not-vacant lot.

Remington and the train that he was in approached like a speeding bullet, as Alice confidently sang through her megaphone:

"O beautiful, for spacious skies,
For amber waves of grain..."

Alice's rendition of 'America the Beautiful' was drowned out by the train's sharp whistle as it got close. Because the people were so close to the tracks, and the train hadn't slowed down at all, the ear-piercing howl of the train was continuous.

As the three railcars rushed by, clattering on the tracks like a hailstorm on a metal roof, tumbleweed was propelled through the little crowd, cowboy hats were dislodged from heads, and the Crowfootians heartily cheered:

"We love you, Mr. Remington!"

"God bless the U.S.A and the second amendment!"

"Thank you for saving our country!"

"Remington, America's best shot!"

"I wouldn't want to live without you!"

And so on.

As the rushing wind died down and the tumbleweed settled, a few Crowfootians shot their pistols into the air. Then a kid's string of firecrackers jarringly popped, which caused Body-builder to drop his plastic bottle and unholster his gun—more than ready to take on the machine gunner that he imagined. Buzzcut grabbed Body-builder's arm and after a few moments was able to get him to lower the weapon. By then, the train was nearly out of sight.

"Can you believe these people?" Buzzcut said to Body-builder, as the cheers continued.

Remington's train had entered and exited the boundaries of Crowfoot during a span of six seconds. That, however, didn't seem to have bothered the Crowfootians. They were used to it. No train had stopped, or even slowed, at Crowfoot in the last 80 years.

"Wow, that was pretty cool," mustached and cowboy-hatted Benson said from his tailgate, to the general vicinity. "I think I saw him wave."

"Me too!" a few folks agreed.

Several were reviewing blurred selfies that they'd taken as the train went by.

"Look!" a little girl said, scampering down the stony slope from the tracks, holding a flattened penny as high as she could.

"Keep that for the rest of your life," Benson said, his voice like a slowly rocking chair on a creaky wooden porch. "That's a special coin."

"Sure is," was the general consensus.

They all watched the train disappear to the east as it gently turned behind a big hill that had three body-sized crosses driven into it. For a moment, in the soft light of dusk as the rain stopped, everyone felt satisfied. Like they'd been a part of, or at least near to, something special. As if they were somehow a little less isolated and more important than before.

But then they heard a terrible and persistent screeching from the east, which sounded like some massive, defiant cyclops being dragged down into Hell. It silenced them all, until Marybeth tentatively declared:

"Well, that didn't sound good."

Buzzcut tried to make a phone call, but it didn't go through.

One of the scarecrow-like teenagers jumped onto his mud-speckled four-wheeler and, before the Secret Servicemen could stop him, raced off toward the hill on the sloppy trail beside the tracks. A few people began to walk that way, following the boy on the four-wheeler.

"Alright, folks," Body-builder sternly said to everyone, hand on his holster. "Stay put."

A couple boys sitting on four-wheelers looked to their parents, who looked to Alice. She subtly nodded her head and so the parents told their sons that they should, as they'd been instructed, stay put. They and everyone else obliged.

"Well, officers," Alice said, loud enough for all to hear, "it sounds like Mr. Remington has come to a halt. How may we assist?"

"By staying put," Body-builder gruffly said.

"There's no damned reception," Buzzcut announced, frustratedly pocketing his phone as he began pacing.

Nervously, the people of Crowfoot talked amongst themselves as Buzzcut and Body-builder argued about what to do and who should do it.

It wasn't long, though, before they all heard the gradually loudening whine of a four-wheeler. Then everyone saw the boy rapidly navigating the ruts and sliding on the sloppy trail. As soon as he had parked amidst the crowd and turned off the engine, he excitedly said:

"It was a mudslide over by Benson's. Covered the tracks, but miraculously the train stopped in time. Everyone is OK. They are headed here on foot. Offered Mr. Remington a ride, but he politely declined. Boy is he something."

"You heard him, folks," Alice said into her megaphone, sending hands up to a few pairs of young, sensitive ears. "Let's prepare a warm Crowfoot welcome!"

And again, all of the Crowfootians cheered.

"I'll go pick them up," Buzzcut said, and took a few steps toward the only vehicle without rust on it: a large, gray SUV.

"I wouldn't do that, if I were you," Benson said.

But Buzzcut didn't listen. He put the vehicle into four-wheel drive and hurriedly drove out of the lot, across Main Street—which was made of old bricks—and onto the muddy two track that followed the train tracks. Everyone watched as in the dark-blue dusk his red taillights slowly advanced. He'd made it about

100 yards, just beyond the village limits, when he came to a slight rise. Buzzcut tried to accelerate and build momentum, to make it to the top of the little hill, but only made it about half-way up before he slid backward. And as he tried to speed back up the hill, the tires of the SUV dug into the mud and then they spun without moving the vehicle. For a while, he continued to press the gas and dig himself deeper into the ruts. Then, he opened the door, looked at what he'd done, and screamed unabashedly:

"F***ck! F*ck! F*ck! F*ck!"

A murmur of horror and disgust spread through the lot.

Benson sternly said to Body-builder: "That's no way to speak in front of children."

Body-builder didn't respond. He jogged off toward the SUV, where it was decided that he should push the vehicle as Buzzcut hit the gas again. They tried, and Body-builder valiantly attempted to justify his muscles. But it didn't work. The only change was that the vehicle got more stuck and Body-builder became covered in mud. The two of them slowly walked back to the lot.

Alice met them when they arrived. It was nearly dark, though Buzzcut and Body-builder could tell that her face had reddened and that her hands were on her hips. She said to Buzzcut:

"Sir, in our community, we don't speak that way in front of children. Now you tell Jenny that you are sorry. And that it was in fact a flock of Mallard ducks that you saw over there and were pointing out, one by one."

"We are technically in the Prairie Pothole region," Benson said. "A duck hotspot. It's feasible."

"Oh, back off," Buzzcut sharply said, his breath rapidly condensing and evaporating on the lenses of his glasses.

Alice suddenly grabbed his bicep with a vice-like grip and fiercely hissed:

"I said to say you are sorry."

Buzzcut and Body-builder both noticed that everyone around them took a single step forward. Like a Python just beginning to tighten its grip. The people stared heavily, without a word, many with heads slightly tilted. Which was unsettling, to say the least.

The little girl rocked from side to side beside Marybeth, her skirt swaying with each movement. She looked down and held her flattened penny by her chest with two hands.

"I'm sorry, honey," Buzzcut managed to say, nervously adjusting his glasses with his free hand. "For a moment there I lost control. I sincerely apologize. It won't happen again. Sometimes ducks come out of nowhere."

Although no one took a step back, the tension there in the center of the crowd seemed to slacken, even if only slightly.

"Jenny," Alice said sweetly, "do you accept the man's apology?"

The little girl nodded, still without making eye contact.

"Apology accepted," Alice said, flipping back her hair after letting go of Buzzcut's arm. "Looks like your boss is on his way."

And so everyone watched as the distant, warm-orange glow of three lanterns bounced with the steps of unseen people.

While the group beside the tracks slowly approached, a single dusk to dawn light hanging at the meeting point of a couple long, crisscrossed wires turned on in the center of town. The light faintly illuminated the intersection beneath it, where the brick road crossed a gravel one that ran about 75 yards to the north of and parallel to the railroad tracks. Every ten or so seconds the light quickly flickered. It was just bright enough to make visible red-bricked 'Marty's General Store,' the small post office, a log-cabin structure called 'The Tavern,' a two-story but narrow church, and a few vacant businesses. One of the abandoned buildings with cloudy windows still had a faded 'Ellie's Sweets' sign above the door. About five one-story residences, all with flaky paint, could also be seen near where the darkness overtook the flickering light.

Remington, along with his group, walked between the rails on sections of wood atop the stone ballast. When he made it to the point where the railroad tracks crossed the brick road, he saw the small crowd that the boy had told him to expect. There were probably about 30 people, he figured. They were gathered in a lot where a couple trucks with headlights on provided some light. Ranchers, mostly. Blue-collar people. The type who'd won him his second term.

"Howdy, folks!" he said, voice strong with a slight southern accent.

There was just enough light for the Crowfootians to see Remington's big, slightly off-center smile as he approached. He was wearing his signature white cowboy hat, dark-blue jeans, and a light-blue shirt with sleeves rolled up on his forearms. In his mid-fifties, Remington was tall, fit, and tan. Out of respect, Alice didn't use the megaphone when he and the three Secret Servicemen with him joined the crowd. But her voice boomed anyway:

"My goodness, Mr. President. I'm Alice, mayor of Crowfoot. Welcome! This here is one of the oldest settlements in our great state. Crowfoot was established way back in 1875."

Remington looked around the lot which was scattered with people, knee-high grass, and tumbleweed, then at the town's center beneath the single, inconsistent light source. And he said to Alice:

"Well, honey, I have to ask. When was it *de*-established?"

And he laughed grandly, like they'd all seen so many times on T.V., then put a hand on Buzzcut's shoulder for support.

For a moment, Alice smiled quietly. Feeling like a stunned boxer after taking an unexpected jab to the face. But she quickly recovered:

"On account of your station and the stress you have endured this evening, Mr. President, I'll let that disrespect slide with a one-time pass."

"Well, Ms. Alice, I appreciate your grace," he

glibly said, with another big smile. "There most certainly has been a fair deal of stress this evening. I know that I'm here to promote the railroad and public transit, but this sure can't be good publicity."

"We won't tell a soul," a rancher from the crowd sincerely said.

"Thank you, sir. That's mighty kind. Exactly what I'd expect from the great state of Wyoming."

The crowd collectively gasped as one of the Secret Servicemen from the train whispered in Remington's ear.

"I mean *Montana*. Montana! Sorry folks, it's been a *long* day."

"Mr. President," Alice said as the crowd murmured, "would you like me to lead you to our community's bed and breakfast? It is a great place to get some rest. I'm sure Eleanor here could help you out."

"Sure could!" said a septuagenarian sitting on a lawn chair, with legs crossed. "We have a presidential rate that I trust you'll like."

"We appreciate the offer," Buzzcut said, "but we already radioed from the train and have arranged for a car to pick us up this evening.

Someone will also remove our vehicle from the mud as soon as possible. Apologies."

"Maybe next time, Eleanor," Remington offered.

"Well," Alice cheerfully said. "Nearest highway is 30 miles distant. So, I guess we've got some time. And I've got some people to introduce you to, Mr. President. We even have a federal employee here! Marybeth, come on over and say hello."

And so, Marybeth, along with her daughter Jenny, came over. Marybeth was wearing her Postal Service uniform.

"Sir," Marybeth said, hands on Jenny's shoulders in front of her. "I want you to know that despite my occupation, I don't harbor any ill will about what you are trying to do to the Service. I'm sure you must have a plan about how to provide rural communities like this with affordable deliveries without the Postal Service."

"Oh, darling," he said, automatically in campaign mode again. "We all know that the USPS is a waste of taxpayer money. But that doesn't mean that there aren't great people working for the Service. Like yourself, I'm sure. I have no doubt that you'll land on your feet when we get the bill through for disbandment.

And then we'll have the means to better help private parcel-delivering companies, to keep their prices down. I bet you'll be at the top of their hiring list."

Marybeth just smiled and nodded as Jenny looked down, the penny still in both hands at her chest.

"Alright, Mr. President," Alice said heartily. "Now you've got to meet—"

"I'm sorry, Miss," Body-builder interrupted, after which the crowd almost imperceptibly constricted even more. "But the president is tired and needs some rest."

"My goodness! What happened to you?" Remington said to Body-builder. "Were you in the mudslide? Speaking of which, I've gotta know. What's going on with that farmhouse up on the hill, right above where the mudslide happened? There's a runoff pipe dumping water right down onto the tracks where the mud is. Which caused the slide, I reckon. That *can't* be up to code."

"But you said that regulations kill jobs," Benson firmly said, and then spit some tobacco juice. "We all went down to Billings last year and heard you say it, in person. There's no code here anymore. Thanks to *you*."

The crowd grumbled in assent and a woman sarcastically asked:

"Did you have that entire train to yourself, Mr. President?"

"I guess there are perks that come with the job," Remington sheepishly replied.

Like a swarming ball of bees trying to keep their center warm, with their queen standing approvingly just slightly off-center, the crowd tightened so that Remington's back pressed against two of his guards. Finally, Buzzcut said:

"Alright, folks, alright. Backup up. Backup *now*. And please, put away your guns."

A young man holding a shotgun above his head, standing on his tailgate, said:

"Has Mr. Remington forgotten about second amendment rights? Out here we take our rights seriously, sir."

"Certainly do!" a handful of others assuredly said.

Everyone knew that the people of Crowfoot had the Secret Servicemen outgunned. Not a single one, though, knew what to do about it.

Buzzcut, Body-builder, and the other Secret Servicemen began shoving people backward and forming a human shield around Remington, who silently stood with his arms crossed. He looked mortified, squarely in the beam of a headlight. His fear seemed to enliven the crowd even more. Everyone began trying to share their two cents at the same time:

"Nobody talks sh*t about Crowfoot!" a boy howled.

"This ain't hippy-dippy Wyoming!" Eleanor screamed.

"The Postal Service is the backbone of our nation!" Marybeth contended.

"Guns protect us from tyrants!" a group of men began to chant.

"Regulations kill ranches!" Benson explained.

The five Secret Servicemen had pushed the people back as far as they could without creating gaps in their human circle. However, the ever-loudening cacophony produced momentary slivers of grievance that still easily made it to Remington, each stinging like buckshot.

Above all the frantic noise, Alice's megaphone-amplified voice firmly instructed:

"Take a deep breath, everyone! Please, a deep breath."

The shoving gradually stopped. The arguing and yelling subsided. And everyone, even Remington, looked to Alice. And she continued to speak through her megaphone, just outside of the ring of Secret Servicemen.

"Look at us. I mean look at us! We are all Americans, for crying out loud. Americans!"

She walked around the circle, glaring at the Secret Servicemen and at her fellow Crowfootians who surrounded them.

"This is no way to treat another American. Not even a liberal. You all should be ashamed. Acting like a bunch of starving coyotes."

She stopped walking and looked directly at Remington for several tense moments, then said:

"I just have this to say to you, Mr. President. Then we will leave you alone. You may be the president of the United States. But I'm mayor of Crowfoot. And I know my people. You best be careful what you go and stir up. Because nothing is more liable to kill ya' than people who love you that you have forgotten. And us out here? Well, we may be forgotten. But you don't mess with Crowfoot, sir. We're everything you claim to stand for. And based on what I've seen this evening, I don't think you can handle that."

"Amen," Benson said. "Let's go to The Tavern while the president waits for his ride."

And without another word the people of Crowfoot all began walking away. They closed their tailgates, turned off their trucks' headlights, folded their chairs, pocketed their flags, pulled up their 'Vote Remington' signs, and left.

Three orange-glowing lanterns provided the sole light that was left there in the dark lot. Only a few trucks, the president, and his men remained. And little Jenny, who stood swaying in her skirt over at the edge of the lot, by the brick street. Just her silhouette was visible, as the light flickered behind her. After his human shield disintegrated, Remington said to her:

"Little lady, do you want an autograph?"

He got a pen from his shirt pocket and began walking toward her. In the distance, the president saw a light in The Tavern turn on. A few moments later, someone also turned on the blue and red 'open' sign in the window—which shined brightly there in the dark—as the last of the Crowfootians began to walk up the porch steps on their way inside.

"Come on, Jenny," Marybeth called from The Tavern's porch, using Alice's megaphone.

Gingerly, the little girl knelt and tentatively placed her flattened penny in a clump of tall grass. Then she pressed it firmly so that the coin disappeared deep within the scratchy stalks and blades. And before Remington could make it to her with his pen, Jenny ran away as fast as she could. He watched her hurry down the slick, brick road beneath the dim light hanging from the wires. The light flashed off for a moment and when it came back on Jenny was at the top of the stairs that led into The Tavern, where Marybeth had been waiting. Marybeth and Jenny went inside and, perfectly framed by the opening and closing of The Tavern's door, Remington heard music from the jukebox and Hank Williams wail: "I'm so lonesome I could cry."

And nearly alone there in the dark, in the almost-again-vacant lot in Crowfoot, Montana, Remington began to shiver.

Looking back to Buzzcut, Body-builder, and the others, he desolately said:

"What's up with these hicks? I mean, they. Well, they..."

And for the first time in a long while, Remington couldn't think of a single thing to say.

*Mongrel*

by

D.B.

An old man in a bath robe walked slowly
despite quick steps across his small, but lush
and perfect, lawn. Just a bit of late-morning
dew still remained on the grass. He approached
the fence that separated his yard from
Belinda's. A small, white dog shrilly barked
from the cement porch behind him.

"Young lady," he said "what in the dickens are
ya' doing?"

Her tightly curled, rust-colored hair held his
attention as he stood beside her, though on his
side of the fence. Then she looked up and
smiled as if she were just pulling weeds. He

noticed that subtle freckles were scattered across her nose and cheeks, just like they had been when she was a kid who stopped by occasionally for ice cream. Which seemed like only a few years ago, though he knew that her childhood must have been longer ago than that.

"My mother put this up," Belinda calmly responded, using wire cutters to slice through another segment of chain link. "And now that I own the place, I can put a hole in this fence if I want to."

"What?" he gruffly asked.

Louder, she said: "It is my fence now and I can do with it what I want."

"But Fluffy will get into your yard."

"I don't mind, Mr. Pelletier," Belinda said, sharply snapping through the fence. "Now she will have two times as much space to play. And I can put a gate in, if you'd like."

Their yards were back-to-back, hers south of his. It just so happened that the properties to the east and the west of Mr. Pelletier's were also bordered by fences. All he had put up were a couple small sections of wooden fence from two corners of his house to his neighbors' fences, to keep Fluffy in his yard.

"You might think otherwise," he said, "when

she settles on a new poopin' ground."

Belinda made her last cut, pulled out the foot-and-half by two section of the fence, and tossed it aside.

She sweetly said: "Come on, Fluffy!"

The little dog leapt off of the porch and, after a moment's hesitation, quickly passed by Mr. Pelletier, trotted through the new door, and let Belinda pet her. Then she began sprinting in circles. She didn't seem to mind that Belinda's lawn was more vegetatively diverse and less lush than Mr. Pelletier's.

"Just let me know if you ever need me to run her back to your side," Belinda said.

Mr. Pelletier's head and shoulders turned together as he watched his little dog continue to run in circles around Belinda's yard. Then he looked at Belinda and resignedly said:

"You're one strange cocktail, honey."

*

"Hey, Jack," Meredith said, with a lovely British accent. "How's your day going?"

Jack was middle-aged, recently unemployed, and was suffering from undiagnosed depression. He looked at Meredith briefly, nodded his head, and then shifted his attention back outside of the window and looked at his front yard. It was his pride and joy, but he and the yard felt empty today.

"I miss her too, you know?" she said.

Jack didn't say anything, just kept looking out the window. He thought: <u>what a nice voice. I love it when she talks to me</u>. But, of course, he couldn't tell her *that*. So, he remained silent.

"Lizzy said that she will come back home at least once a month," Meredith said, "And just think of all the fun she is having down there."

That didn't seem to cheer him up.

"Want to go for a walk?"

"Sure do," he said.

\*

"You're up early," Belinda said as she walked into the living room, yawning.

Her new roommate, Bullet, was bent almost like a 'u' on the couch. His feet, in black boots, were on the coffee table. He was pale like slightly dirty snow and had shaved his head except for a spiky, black mohawk.

"Yeah, well, that old fuddy Mr. Pelletier sure

does like his opera music. Woke me up at 7:00 or so this morning. I don't much care for that guy, or his yappy little dog."

"I love Fluffy! And once you get to know Mr. Pelletier, he's a sweetheart," Belinda said, as she sat on the recliner. "Hard of hearing, though, which I think explains the loud music. Earplugs will help. Speaking of which, how was the show?"

"Oh, you know," Bullet said. "We killed it."

"How many people showed up?"

"There were *several,*" he replied, after a bit of thought. "But for the best space-punk-metal band in Toronto, not nearly enough. I think the crowds will begin to grow after our new marketing plan begins to take effect."

"Oh yeah," Belinda said, "what's that?"

"Banners. On the outfield fences of Little League fields here in the 'burbs. We got one up over at Chesterfield last night after the show. Under cover of darkness."

"Don't you think, you know, someone will notice? You are supposed to pay for those, I think."

"I'm not worried about it," he very casually said. "And if we get caught, it will just help to build our brand as rule-breakers. Soon they are all going to know who Bullet and the Screams are."

Belinda decided not to ask what target audience Bullet and his band were going for. She got up and took six steps, which brought her to the kitchen and its aquamarine appliances that for some reason her mom had liked.

"Want some popcorn?"

"I'm on a cleanse," he replied.

As the pops slowly started, she sat at the bar that separated the living room from the kitchen. It was strange having someone else in the house. It had always been just her and her mom. The place was, of course, as small as it had been when her mom was around, and the creaks in the walls were the same, but somehow the house wasn't cozy like it used to be.

"So, why do you go by 'Goose'?" Bullet asked.

"I made it up. It's short for mongoose."

"But what about mongoose?" he said, with an exaggerated turn of his head. "Why would you want to be called an abbreviated version of *that*?"

"Because they're fierce," she said "and they are from Africa, like my dad. The mean kids back in school used to call me 'mongrel.' For perhaps obvious reasons. My mum was white, my dad is black. So, reeling mind you, I said to those kids when I was five or so: 'I'm not a mongrel, I'm a mongoose.' And ever since I've gone by Goose."

"I dig it," he said.

For a while, the only sound in the house was creaking from the pipes and popping from the microwave.

"Got any plans for the day?" Bullet finally asked. "Besides popcorn?"

"Not really," she replied, as the pops slowed and the microwave began beeping. "I think I might take the streetcar downtown before my shift starts. Which reminds me. If you ever want free food from Snyder's, I'm your girl."

"The cleanse, remember? Thanks, though."

*

Since their girl Lizzy had gone to college, Jack felt like things had become stale at home and that he needed something new. In a moment of passion, he left Meredith. There was a cute little thing down the road who, all of a sudden, he just had to have. It was the chase he enjoyed, but soon that was over and he had nothing to show for his foolishness. He regretted his actions almost immediately, but there was no way back to Meredith so far as he could tell. One thing led to another and now he found himself in a dreadful hotel. The neighbors were noisy, breakfast was terrible, one of the room-keepers seemed like trouble, and the place had an overbearing stench. But there was nothing much he could do about it now. He had made his bed and so had to sleep in it. As he was lying there in the dark, missing Meredith and feeling terrible, he felt something on his left shoulder and thought: <u>My God, was that a flea?</u>

*

"53 times!"

"What was that?" Belinda asked the middle-aged, heavy-set woman with curly and wild orange hair who sat beside her in the trolley, reading from a tablet.

"That's how many times a poor fellow over in the States was shot by the cops. On account of being black, I'm sure."

Belinda didn't say anything, just looked out the window that was only about an inch from her nose. In the reflection, she could see that a tear was somehow already running down her cheek.

"Oh," the woman said, a little embarrassed. "You've got nothing to worry about, honey. That sort of thing could never happen here. But if I were you, I wouldn't go to the U.S."

About 30 blocks before she'd planned to, Belinda pulled the cord. As she eagerly waited for the trolley to stop, she dabbed her eyes with a tissue. Today, she needed to feel some love before another dreadful nine hours at Snyder's. And there was only one place she knew where she could get it.

*

"Hey, Goose!" the young guy at the front desk said. He was a volunteer at the shelter. Kind of cute.

"Hi Chad," Belinda said. "Got any new pups, today?"

"I'm not sure," he replied, "head on back there and Gretchen will get you hooked up."

As usual, she quickly walked through the cat section as they glared at her. She pushed open the heavy, swinging doors that led into the dog area.

"Hey, Gretchen. How's it going?"

"Oh, hey Goose," Gretchen said, putting down a bag of kibble. She was about 30 and took her job very seriously. "Just got done feeding the pack."

The room was about 200 feet long by 50 feet wide and on both sides of a narrow walkway were twenty compartments that each held a single dog. One of them was barking incessantly.

"Anyone you think I should meet this morning?" Belinda asked.

"Well," Gretchen said, leading Belinda to the end of the corridor, "we just got a purebred German Shepherd. The rest are just mongrels."

Belinda felt her face flush, though remained quiet.

"So, what do you think?" Gretchen asked. "Want to play with Archie?"

They both watched him. Archie was a beautiful, nearly all-black 'teenager,' as Belinda's mom would have said, who was furiously gnawing on a bone and not paying any attention to Belinda or Gretchen.

"He's handsome," Belinda said, "but I think I'd like to meet someone else this morning."

"Alright, girl, just let me know."

Gretchen went into a supply closet and Belinda

began to slowly make her way past each of the dogs. First, there was Sonic, a beagle-like mix who piercingly yipped over and over. Then there was Roxy—big, old, and yellowish—who was curled up in a far corner with her back to everyone. Checkers, just a little bigger than a Chihuahua, took a treat from Belinda, sniffed her fingers, and then trotted off through the door in the back of his room for some privacy. Belinda introduced herself to several more dogs, giving treats to most, and finally made it to the cage furthest from the German Shepherd. There, she saw Morrison. He sat in the middle of his compartment. His floppy ears were alert as he looked straight at her. His legs were short and his body was long; his fur was all shiny-black except for his chest, which was white. There was just a bit of gray on his muzzle and he had a striking dignity about him. Belinda kneeled, but Morrison didn't seem very much affected. His dark-brown eyes, though, began to show a little less suspicion as they stared at her. Despite her requests, he didn't move.

"So beautiful," she said to herself.

"Did you find someone you want to play with yet?" Gretchen said, from down the corridor.

"Yes, I think so."

Gretchen began walking toward Belinda. As she got close, she said:

"Oh, I don't think this is the one for you, Belinda. Morrison nearly bit a guest yesterday. And he doesn't seem to like to play, anyway."

And, as if on cue, he began a low and formidable growl.

"Come on, Mr. Morrison," Belinda said, in a sing-songy voice. "All work and no play makes Jack a dull boy."

Morrison inquisitively turned his head sideways, wagged for just a moment, and took a few small, tentative steps toward Belinda. She put a pinkish-red treat through the gate and he took it. Then he laid down like an arrow, his chin on his paws, and his nose just a few inches from Belinda's outstretched fingers. She could feel his breath as she kept talking to him. Slowly, his bushy tail began to wag more and more.

"You've already signed the waiver, haven't you?"

"Yes, I have," Belinda said, in the same cheery voice she'd been using for Morrison.

"Alright, I'll get a leash. I'll bring him to you outside in the play pen."

As she walked toward the play pen, Belinda heard a single, long whine from Morrison's cage.

Like she had done probably fifty times before, Belinda went outside and sat on the long bench in the small, fenced-in area that was completely shaded by a giant oak. And after a few moments, Gretchen came out with Morrison. He carefully positioned himself about as far away from Gretchen as he could be, without pulling on the leash, as he casually sniffed some leaves.

"Alright, Goose, you know the drill. Just push the buzzer when you are done and I'll come get him."

Gretchen took off Morrison's leash and left the two alone.

"Why don't you come up by me?" Belinda asked, patting the wooden seat of the bench that she sat on.

Without hesitation, Morrison jumped right up on the bench, laid down, and put his chin on Belinda's thigh. She kept talking to him, and his tail wagged slowly but persistently. She threw a ball and he briefly lifted his head to look at it. But he was happy where he was and, really, so was she. He put his chin back on her thigh. They sat there together in the warm shade for a long time. Until Belinda could no longer convince herself to leave the shelter without him.

*

"I hope you have a big yard," Chad said, as she filled out the last of the paperwork. "He likes to run. Not play, exactly. But he likes to run."

"I do," she said, just after an idea occurred to her. <u>Or at least, I will soon.</u>

"Great. I was afraid no one would take him. That German Shepherd will be gone in a week. But older dogs like Morrison, sometimes no one ever takes them."

Belinda looked down at Morrison, who was sitting beside her. Panting in a way that made it look like he was smiling. She handed the paperwork to Chad and felt happier than she had in a long time.

"You're not going to stop visiting me?" Chad asked. "Now that you finally got yourself a pup."

"I'll see you around, Chad," she said.

Morrison walked right next to her as they went out the door. She looked at her phone and saw the time.

"Well, sh*t," she said. "I'd better call in sick."

And so, she did. The scolding that she got didn't dampen her spirits even a bit as she and Morrison walked home.

*

Morrison sat on Belinda's loveseat, looking intently out the living room window. He'd jumped right up there almost immediately after they walked through the door and had yet to leave that spot.

"There they are!" Belinda said, from a closet.

She came into the living room with the wire cutters that she had been looking all over for. Morrison turned to look at her, his heart fluttered, and then he looked back out the window. There were at least three squirrels within view. And he thought he might have seen Lizzy, for just a moment, way on the other side of the street.

"Well, what do you think?" Belinda asked. "Want to see your new back yard? It is about to double in size. I think you'll like Fluffy. She's a doll."

But Morrison was so struck by the new view and neighbors that he didn't follow her when she went out the backdoor with the wire cutters. He did, however, find himself thinking: what a nice voice. I love it when she talks to me.

# ABOUT THE AUTHORS

Dustin Brewer (D.B.) is a conservation biologist who enjoys wild words as much as the wildlife that he studies. His first novel, *Slip or Jump*, was published in 2014. Dustin lived in Michigan with his wife and their mighty mongrel when these stories were written. Learn more at dustywords.com.

Olympia Bernes (O.B.) is a jill of many trades, dabbling in some visual and literary arts, field sciences, and the craft of exploration. You can find her gallivanting around Minnesota looking for a timely bird to photograph or a keen inspiration to write.

Jacob Brewer (J.B.) is an aspiring artist who primarily identifies as a songwriter. But even so, he occasionally dabbles in the writing of fiction and poetry. He's currently located in the greater Tribeca area, where he performs open mics when time permits.

www.ingramcontent.com/pod-product-compliance
Lightning Source LLC
Chambersburg PA
CBHW022040170626
46808CB00003B/1295